For Cathy

Many Blessings

Gillian Brown

ANCIENT CIRCLE

GILLIAN BROWN

For information:

Brown Books
P.O. Box 1331
Redway, CA 95560   USA
707-923-4139

ACKNOWLEDGMENTS

This book is dedicated to my daughter, Gwyn, who helped in its creation. May she grow up strong with the wisdom of the ancient ones.

It is also dedicated to the countless numbers of women who were killed as witches. May this atrocity never be repeated in human history.

I would like to thank Holly Sweet for her cover illustration, and David Katz for his computer wizardry and boundless patience.

1

A silence blanketed the moonless night. Millions of stars blinked and sparkled across the dark cloak of the obsidian sky. A warm summer breeze blew gently through the ancient oak forest, sending a shiver and a whisper through the leaves. From deep within the forest flickered a light. It was the light of a bonfire as its flames danced in the soft wind, casting shadows on the ancient trees. All around the fire, dark figures sat, their faces glowing in the heat of the crackling wood, as the flames danced and flickered. It was the night of the summer solstice, and the women of the village were celebrating the turning of the wheel of the year. The youngest of them was the tiny baby, Kelsey, daughter of June. The oldest of them was the wise woman, Tamar, whose knowledge and power was known throughout the lands. Ivy had sat with her mother through many of these solstice celebrations, and had felt the warmth and companionship of the women surrounding her throughout her years. They lived in the village of Stoneleigh, along the Lifford River.

"Earth my body, water my blood, air my breath, and fire my spirit," sang the priestess Marlea, breaking the silence of the magical night and the voices of the women young and old joined her in the chant, giving thanks for the beauty and power of the earth and its elements.

Ivy had awakened early that morning, and with excitement had jumped up from her cozy sheep skin bed, remembering that today was the day of the great celebration. The morning air was soft and gentle, as the breeze blew in through the open window. She had many things to do in preparation for the events of the day. Her mother was already up and baking delicious oaten bread, and their neighbor Forest had come by with a bundle of willow for the decorations of the feast table. Ivy could smell the warm, delicious bread as it emerged from the oven. It made her body glow with the feeling of good food and excellent company.

"Good morning to you, Ivy," said her mother, whose name was Elspeth. "Did you sleep well on this, the shortest night of the year?"

"Yes, mother, I did," said Ivy, "but can sleep no more. There is water to fetch and flowers to pick for the day." But then a look of fear and apprehension grew across the young girl's face. "Mother," she whispered. "Do you think the black robes will try to stop our celebrations, today? Remember how last year...?"

"Hush," said her mother. "This is a day for happiness and giving thanks, not for sad thoughts, Ivy. The priests can say what they will, this day will never be forgotten or ignored. For this is the great day when the cycles of the earth turn and spring to summer shifts. They will soon recognize the error of their ways, and that the spirits of this earth smile when we celebrate their goodness, not scowl and chide us for not being inside those dark little places they call 'church'. The forest and the riverside are the perfect places for celebration, not those dark, cold places created by those men. How could they think they could ever create something as splendid and magnificent as the trees and the waters? What nonsense! Now, Ivy my dear, run along and fetch me a pail of water. There are roots to wash."

Ivy went out into the morning light and made her way down to the stream from which the villagers drew their water. The morning air smelled fresh and moist. She was excited at the thought of the day's celebrations, but could not dispel the thoughts that the rituals and feast might be disrupted by the priests who had built the small daub and wattle church down in the next valley. Their ways were different from those of the villagers of Stoneleigh. Ivy had heard her mother and their neighbors speaking late into the night of this new religion that the black robes had brought to the land. From what she gathered from their talk, it seemed that the black robes believed there to be just one god, not the many gods and goddesses, spirits and deva that the villagers knew to abound. The black robes also spoke of a special man they called Christ who was a healer and a teacher. "He must have been the sorcerer and medicine bringer of his peoples," thought Ivy as she bent down to scoop the sparkling clear water up into her bucket. "What is wrong with that?" she pondered. "All peoples must have their enchanterers and wise ones. But something is amiss. Why should the black robes feel so strongly that our earth celebrations are wrong and evil?"

The thought bothered her as she made her way up from the stream. But it was soon forgotten as she started to hear the sounds of laughter and merriment from the cottagers, who were spilling outdoors to weave flowers into garlands, to bake bread and prepare foods, to air out their holiday garments, and to get all that was needed to be made ready for this, the celebration of the summer solstice. People were singing merrily and there was laughter and excitement in the air. The people of Stoneleigh toiled in the fields all year and were glad to celebrate the fruits of their labor. The fields were planted and the summer sun now warmed the earth. All thoughts of trouble and conflict left Ivy's mind as she carried the pail of water into her cottage. This was a day for celebration, not strife.

Waiting at the door of Ivy's cottage was her friend Rose.

"Hey, Ivy," Rose called merrily. "Look at the beautiful colors that I have gotten from the plants we gathered yesterday."

Rose showed Ivy a length of dyed wool that was in her basket. Rose's father was one of the finest dyers and weavers of the area. His work was known for miles around and some said it had even been marketed as far north as Hibernia. It was one of Ivy's favorite pastimes to gather flowers, herbs and wild fungi with Rose and her father Finn and then watch the water of the dye pot turn miraculous colors as the plants bathed in it. They were then able to turn the dull, coarse, woven fabric their mothers and fathers spun into the glowing hues of gold, ochre and rust. Ivy stopped to admire the fabric that Rose had brought to show her when a cry rang out. "Neighbors come quick, the black robes have come!" A shiver of fear went through Ivy's body.

2

A tall man in a black cloak sat astride a gray stallion, looming down on the crowd of villagers that had gathered. Ivy could tell from his stern expression that what he had to say was going to be unpopular with the people of her village. She crept closer to the gathered group, so as to hear what the black robe had to say to her people.

"People of Stoneleigh," he commanded. "You have been warned! These pagan rituals have to cease! Anyone discovered in possession of pagan objects or in the forest at night runs the risk of being prosecuted by the holy church ordinance as signed by his holiness the Archbishop of Allbury. I warn you! Your ways are blasphemy and we will no longer tolerate them!" With this he jerked the reins of his horse and headed off across the heath.

The villagers stood in stunned silence. Their rituals for the turning of the wheel of the year had been part of the tradition of the village from time immemorial. The oldest people of the village remembered their grandparents talk of the great celebrations. It seemed as though there had never been a time when these rites had not been practiced.

Jeb the carpenter was the first to speak. " The evil of the black robes grows. We must not take this matter lightly. It is time to consult the old woman of the forest." A mutter of agreement spread through the crowd and four of the villagers broke off from the group to visit the wise woman Tamar.

Tamar lived in a small hut in the forest. She had been there as long as anyone in the village could recall. Ivy always loved going to visit Tamar. Her hut was full of the most exquisite and delicious smells, as aromatic concoctions bubbled on the fire, and herbs and flowers hung from the roof beams to dry. Tamar's shelves were always stocked with pots and jars of different infusions, decoctions, teas, salves and ointments, all with special, sometimes magical, healing properties. Tamar was one of the most respected members of the village community. People from far and wide came to ask Tamar's advice on various ailments, or for strong herbs to strengthen the body or calm the mind. Tamar welcomed them all into her humble abode and worked hard day and night to be of service to her community. It was even rumored that a servant was once sent from the lord of the manor when his wife was experiencing problems in childbirth, to ask for a remedy from Tamar. The villagers knew that Tamar's work was complete when the announcement came from the manor that the lord's wife had given birth to healthy twins and that the mother was recovering.

Ivy was eager to hear what Tamar would say about the threats of the black robes. But she knew that it was not her place to meddle in the affairs of the adults of the village, and that she must wait patiently to hear the results of their conference with Tamar. So she headed back to her family cottage, upset that the day's celebrations had been so seriously marred by the arrival of the black robe. But then she remembered the words of her mother that morning and knew that the celebrations would go on as they had from time immemorial. The powers of earth's shifting and the turning of the seasons would never be changed because of the words of a few impassioned men whose beliefs were different.

Ivy went into her cottage and told her mother of the morning's events. Once more her mother was reassuring, and told Ivy, "All the black robes on earth could not stop the shifting of the seasons, and who could stop the joy we feel in our hearts when these miracles of nature occur? No, Ivy, we may have to change what we do in our celebrations, or maybe where we do them, but that experience can never be erased from our hearts. And as long as people walk on this earth there will be people to come together and celebrate the abundance of this place we call our home. Now, come along, let's put the bread in the oven."

Meanwhile, the group of villagers had arrived at the home of Tamar. "What brings you to my door, fellow villagers?"

asked Tamar as she stepped through her doorway, her cat Shadow slinking softly behind her.

"We have come to seek your advice, Tamar," spoke Joan Brody, the miller. "Do you know of what I speak?"

"Ah, yes, of course," said Tamar. "I have foreseen that this is the last year that there will be dancing on the common, and that the garlands will no longer hang from the bower by the stream. The ways of the world are changing my friends. A new way now spreads o'er the land, a way different from our own, but one that contains an important message. Things will change, my friends, they will change."

"But what can we do, Tamar? What can we do? We cannot stand by and see our celebrations destroyed and our lives altered. This is a sacred time. We must express our thanks for the fertility of the soil and the sun that blesses it or who knows what will happen to the harvest. It is no mere fun and games. We must keep to our rituals that have been passed down through the generations or we shall perish," spoke Will the tanner.

"The ways of the world are many and strange," replied Tamar. "This is a new time and to try to stop it is like trying to stop the winter winds. My friends, you would do well to mark my words. Celebrate and give thanks, yes, but to do so in the old ways will bring a wrath down upon us the like of which you cannot imagine. I suggest you stay in your homes today and give thanks for the turning of the year in your hearts, but do not go to the sacred stone circle, or to the bower by the stream, for there you will meet with danger. The times are changing, my friends, the times are changing. And the signs are that these changes will be with us a while. A long while. Longer than any of our lives, or our children's lives, or our children's children." With these words Tamar shuffled back into her little hut with a curious look on her face. But as she was about to disappear into her home, she suddenly turned and drew herself upright and a power seemed to o'ertake her as she spoke in a voice now more serious and grave. "But tell the other women of Stoneleigh that their time has come. We shall meet in the forest as sunset. Tell them to bring the potions of strength. We will not face this night unprepared. And we will not face the future without summoning all the forces we can to protect and preserve the ancient ways."

The group of villagers stood shocked and alarmed by Tamar's words. It was Matt the weaver who spoke first. "Black robes or not, I intend to decorate the bower as my family has always done and my mother and grandmother before me. And I will challenge any newcomer in black if he dares stop me. And my wife will also stand and fight as did the warrior woman Boudicca whose legions rose against the Roman hordes." With that he drew his dagger from his belt.

"No, Matt," spoke Harry the carpenter. "I think in this you are wrong. I will not risk the safety of myself and my family. We shall not go to the stream or the circle. It is said that the black robes have friends in high places who will defend them and in the village of Almsbury three men were killed who tried to stop the black robes from building their church on top of Weatherall Hill. That must not happen here. I will celebrate the day in my home. I'll not venture forth and risk my life. I have three young ones to think of. But I will consult with Meagan my wife, for it is she who has the final say." Mutters of agreement spread throughout the company. "And what did Tamar mean when she said that their time had come? What is it that the women will do to stop the black robes? What, oh what?" A shudder of fear passed through the crowd, as Harry's question lingered in the stillness of the morning air, now turned chill by the growing thunderheads that were rising from the east.

3

The hot bread was ready and the next thing to be done was to carry the garlands to the riverside. To the people of Stoneleigh the spirit of the water was one of special significance, for it is the bringer and sustainer of all life. Without it no human could ever survive, neither crop grow nor animal thrive. So part of their celebrations always incorporated a visit to the river and a dedication in honor of this powerful element. Ivy gathered the wreaths from the ceiling of the cottage where they had been hanging to dry and headed out of the door. Everything seemed normal again. The children were playing on the heath and other villagers were preparing the long tables for the feast that always followed the day's ritual and celebration.

Ivy headed down the path through the forest and to the water's edge. As she scooped up the water with her pail she saw the reflection of her shining face in the shallow, emerald pool beneath her. Watching the water ripple and swirl, she caught a glimpse of something that took her breath away. She looked again and could just make out something glistening in the water like the back of a shiny fish but with the radiance of the moon. In the glimmer of the reflection, she sat and breathed deep. She could feel a power growing inside her and caught her breath as a voice emerged from the depths, "Ivy....Ivy.....Ivy." The startled girl braced her body in concentration to receive this message, this voice that was emerging from another world. She strained to hear the voice, both faint and ethereal. "Speak, write and all will be told. Speak, write and all will be told. Speak, write and all..." The voice drifted into faintness as the sound of the rushing water overcame it. Ivy sat back on the grassy bank, her head swimming from the intoxication of the power she felt as the voice reached into her consciousness. She felt both a sense of wonder and awe, but also the shudder of fear rippled through her body. What did it mean?

As she turned to walk back up the path she was startled by a figure that loomed above her, all in black. It was a man who bore the familiar silver cross around his neck. It was one of the black robes. Yet this was a young man and he did not have the stern expression of the man she had seen earlier that day on the stallion. He, too, was startled by the appearance of the other. Ivy looked down and tightened the grasp on her bundle as she tried to hurry by the man. But she was surprised by a soft voice that spoke out to her, "Excuse me, miss. I mean no harm. I was just sent to survey the area for my lord the bishop. It is told that wicked and evil things occur in this forest. But I can see nothing amiss. Where do you live young one?" The voice was soft and as smooth as newly churned butter. But Ivy was not to be fooled. His very dress was enough to arouse suspicion in her. He was obviously a spy, seeking to make trouble for her people.

"I am from yonder village, sir, and if you'd pardon me, I'd best be on my way," she stammered.

"I wish not to hinder you, but would you kindly tell me, what is it that the villagers do when they gather here?" said the soft syrup-like voice. Ivy could not help herself, she so badly wanted to leave, but his kind questions led her to want to reply.

"We come to give thanks, that is all, to give thanks," she stuttered in response. And with that, her heart pounding, she ran off down the path. She did not stop or turn back until she was safe in view of the village. She could hear the cantering of hooves and saw the young black robe riding off into the distance. She felt troubled in her mind as she thought of what she had told the young priest, but she also felt a sense of pride for her people and their rituals and did not want to have to hide in fear.

There was great commotion in the house when Ivy returned from the river. One of her neighbors was talking in a soft but troubled voice about what Tamar had recommended. Elspeth was very upset and Ivy could tell that they had different opinions about how to respond to the threats of the black robes. Some of the other villagers were there too, and no one could really be heard as everyone was talking at once. One thing that Ivy knew for sure though was that whatever was going on was deadly serious, as she could see her mother pulling down a heavy chest from the rafters, the one that held her ceremonial robes and regalia. Ivy had only seen these things used once before, at a time when a great pestilence was sweeping the land and great spells had to be cast to protect the village. In the trunk was Elspeth's robe of power that she had woven herself in wool dyed by special roots and fungi that Tamar had brought to the house in a veil of secrecy. When Elspeth draped the cloak around her shoulders it seemed to change her very nature, for she became incredibly powerful and seemed infused by a wisdom and strength that was remarkable. Ivy was proud of her mother's abilities as one of the wise women of the village, and hurried over to the stool to help her mother drag the trunk to the ground. The other villagers knew its meaning too and there was a strange hush in the room now as if the answers to their questions had settled on them as did the dust that hung in the air.

"It is time for action, not words, my friends," said Elspeth as she pulled a strangely gnarled piece of wood from the chest. It was the first time Ivy had seen this object up close and now she saw that it had been carved with a writhing snake-like figure whose eyes were small, amethyst crystals that had been inlaid into the wood. There was also a strange inscription on the staff in curious lettering, which when Ivy thought about it she realized she had seen somewhere once before, but could not quite remember where. The staff seemed incredibly old and as the morning sun shone into the window of the cottage its light flooded across the room and the eyes of the serpent on the staff glistened and flashed as if with a life of its own.

"When the sun reaches its zenith we shall meet at the stones, dear friends. Spread the word throughout the village, we shall meet at the stones," said Elspeth as she planted the staff firmly on the ground next to her, and drew the cloak of power firmly around her shoulders.

4

At noon a crowd of villagers was to be seen on its way up the spiral path that led to the circle of stones at the top of Lammas Hill. The stones were an imposing sight and could be seen from many miles in every direction. It was known that they were thousands of years old and had been placed there on top of the hill as a directional marker of the lines that crossed the landscape, and were of a type of stone that was not common to that area, but had been dragged to this spot from afar. There was a special quality to these stones that made them particularly suited to their purpose and they stood ten feet high in a circle that was at least forty feet across. Ivy had heard tell of similar stone circles all across the country and it was told that across the waters in Gaul there were rows of standing stones that ran for miles across the landscape. The stone circle of Lammas Hill was the site for special ceremonies and celebrations and to stand in their midst at sunset created a sense of awe and wonder and a sensation of the mystery of life on the earth. Ivy remembered the last time she had been up at the stone circle. It was at Beltane, the spring celebration, when a blessing of thanks was given to the earth for its bounty. Ivy had been honored with the position of flower maiden on that day and had carried bundles of daffodils, symbol of spring time ripeness, to the circle. Ivy felt herself grow sad at the thought that this specially-called gathering at the circle at noon was needed not to prepare for a ceremony or ritual, but to discuss whether ceremony and ritual were even possible today. She huddled close to her mother as Elspeth strode up the spiral path, her cloak flying from her shoulders like wings, her gnarled staff planting itself firmly and strongly into the earth as they walked.

Once at the top of the hill, the villagers formed into a single file and entered the circle at the eastern doorway created by the henges and bowed their heads in respect for this ancient place. A few were heard to mutter a blessing or prayer for guidance as they entered the inner circle. Then they crowded together in a circle and waited silently for several minutes before beginning the meeting.

Will the tanner was the first to speak. " The word comes from Tamar that our rituals must not happen as usual today, that our safety is threatened if we do so. But we all know that we must give thanks to the earth for her abundance or how will our crops grow and thrive? I say we continue as before or the wrath of the earth will be ten times greater than that of these black robes. For who is it that has more power? Man or the spirits of the earth?" There was a mumble of agreement in the crowd.

Then Jan the woodsman spoke, " My brother married into the clan on the north bank of the Rellon River, and a group of black robes came in there last autumn and burnt down the flower bower that those folk had at a sacred spring. And the desecration did not stop there. They had the miller arrested for attacking the black robe's leader, one they call bishop, and nothing has been heard of him since. These people have friends in high places. We must be so careful my friends, so careful. My heart says we meet in secrecy and hide our ways from them that could harm us. The spirits will hear our songs, chants and rituals whether we be in the sacred grove or inside the mead hall. We can post guards outside the hall and be forewarned if any black robes are snooping around." Many of the villagers mumbled in agreement. But the murmurs and chatter suddenly came to an abrupt halt as an almighty roar rang out from the eastern side of the circle as Elspeth struck her staff into the ground and cried out with a piercing scream that sounded like the cawing of a raven. "Enough!" she cried. "It is time for the circle to be cast. Whichever way our path leads today friends, we must be protected! It is time to cast the circle of protection around us friends. The time is now. The hour is getting late." And with that the piercing cries of a dozen or more women of the village rang through the air, and these women stepped forwards from the crowds to join Elspeth in the inner circle. Ivy was amazed to see that they too were all wearing cloaks of the same woven colors as her mother's and had tall commanding staffs of oak with them also. Ivy had been to many rituals in her time but had never seen these women working with such power and seriousness. The crowd grew hushed as the women began to chant an opening incantation to draw the powers of the east, south, west and north in, and then circle around, pointing their staffs to the four directions repeating a chant over and over at each direction. Ivy's skin bristled with both fear and excitement at seeing this, a most special form of magical protection.

As if the powers that were being drawn in were too powerful for them, one by one the villagers started to crouch closer to the ground and Ivy could see that they were receiving the words of the chant and were starting to repeat it over and over, over and over, to summon up the forces of the earth to protect them and the work they were about to do. The stones themselves seemed to resonate with the sounds of the people and it was as if the ancient stone temple was aglow with the heat and the fire of the magic that the people wove. One of the women stumbled to the ground as if in trance, others whirled around like wild, frenzied beings and others held their arms aloft, staff in hand, chanting and crying to the sky. Ivy bowed her head in deep reverence for this magic, for this moment, for this opportunity to protect the ways of her people. Many of the children had been left at home with the elder ones, so Ivy felt a true glow of thankfulness in her heart for the gift of this time. Then a hush fell on the group and Elspeth pulled a pouch from her belt and poured a mixture into the palm of her left hand. She took a pinch of the mixture and cast it to the east, then another which she cast to the south and so on round the circle. The other women sat down on the ground together in a circle and pointed outward, looking up at the sky. Elspeth then began to speak in an ancient tongue, one from a place beyond any of their lives. She was casting a spell of protection around herself, her family, her village and its people. The villagers sat with their eyes closed in humble silence until Elspeth was finished. The women in the center circle then stood up and started moving in a snake-like rhythmic pattern in the opposite direction from that of before and then slowed to a stop.

Elspeth, whose eyes flashed with the power, spoke, "The circle of protection is cast. Tamar has spoken that the women meet again at sunset to complete the spell. It is now time for us to choose whether to stand our ground and celebrate this the solstice as we have from time immemorial or whether to change our ways to suit the newcomers. What will it be, friends? Will we stand our ground or shall we hide in fear?" Ivy could see that her mother's feet were planted so firmly in the ground that they might soon take root.

The cry rang out, "We will stand! We will stand!" And soon the whole crowd was shouting it. The magic of the circle, the ancient power of the stones and the spells cast had imbued the villagers with a strength and courage that was unanimous and complete.

"So, my friends, then let us begin. To the bower let us now go. It is time to celebrate!" Thus spoke Elspeth and the crowd began to turn and head out of the stone circle, their prayers cast, their hearts full, as Ivy ran to her mother and hugged her and held her.

"Ivy, Ivy my child," said Elspeth with the voice of a mother not a priestess. "It is time for me to pass on this cloak of wisdom to you my daughter. You must learn these spells and these chants. They must now pass on to you just as my mother passed them on to me and her mother before her. The circle must not break. This is now your time. What you and those others of your days do with these teachings is so very important. The times are indeed changing, my love. I will teach you all I know."

And arm in arm, Ivy and her mother made their way down the spiral path, the voices of the spirit pounding in their hearts.

5

The day's celebrations usually began with a parade, so the villagers hurried themselves towards their crofts and cottages to dress in their holiday garments and to collect their ribbons, musical instruments and flags for the parade. As the families began to gather on the heath, Ivy and her friend Rose attached bells to their ankles and wrists so that they could join in the rhythm and songs with the other musicians. The parade began with Tom the tumbler jumping and twirling and singing a merry song. The villagers joined in behind him and soon another snake could be seen winding its way across the fields of Stoneleigh, this one vibrant with the colors of bright holiday garments and waving banners and flags. There was Mary who played a drum and Sarah with a wooden penny whistle. Ivy and Rose danced and twirled in merriment as the procession wound its way down to the creekside. Elspeth was no longer wearing her cloak of power, but was wearing a long, richly dyed lichen green dress of finely spun wool. She had a garland of flowers and herbs on her head. The crowd arrived at the stream and gathered around the bower that was now bedecked with beautiful garlands of flowers from the gardens and forests, hills and valleys of the area. Beneath the bower an altar had been set with glowing rocks, carvings, sculptures and candles and many other special offerings of the people of Stoneleigh. More rounds of songs followed and then the villagers lined up along the side of the stream and cast petals and leaves into the clear flowing water with a wish or a prayer for the sustenance of the water and the life it brings. The crowd became stilled and quiet and many bowed their heads in reverence and respect for the divinity of the water.

From there the villagers dispersed and headed back to the heath. But Ivy lingered a while at the water's edge, her mind now filled with the memory of the voice she had heard speaking to her from the water. "What did it mean?" she wondered, "Speak, write? I do not know how to write, very few people do. So what did it mean?" She sat for quite a while at the stream and then suddenly awoke from her deep thoughts and realized that she was the last one there and must head back to the heath for the games. She turned and headed back up the bank to the path through the forest. As she ducked under a fallen oak branch she thought she heard a noise. It sounded like a wounded animal or a child crying in pain. The noise sounded like it came from over behind a big rock. So Ivy went to investigate. The whimpering noise stopped and a deep groan could be heard. This time it didn't sound like a child, but a full grown man. Ivy's breath quickened as a warm flow of fear trembled through her body.

She felt suddenly chilled and gathered her shawl closer around her as the forest seemed to grow suddenly darker as clouds moved in steadily, blocking the sun. Ivy decided to move slowly and hide behind a very large, ancient oak tree, so that she could remain hidden, but could peek carefully through its branches to see who was there. To her astonishment she could see that there was a man collapsed on the forest floor beneath the big rock. Ivy could see a thin trickle of blood running from his forehead, and then with fright, realized that it was the young black robe, the spy. What was she to do? What was he doing there? It seemed that he was badly injured and in no position to harm her, so taking a deep breath of courage, Ivy grabbed a large oak branch that had fallen in a storm for protection and stepped out from behind the tree. "What has happened? Can you hear me?" she spoke in the firmest voice she could muster. But the man only groaned, so Ivy stepped closer.

The man's eyes fluttered open and with great pain and agony he mumbled. "I slipped from the rock. I hit my head. I need help. Help me." With that he slipped back into unconsciousness. The man was in very bad condition. "I'd better fetch help," thought Ivy, and covering the young man with the silver cross with her shawl, she ran back to find her mother. She would know what to do.

6

Ivy ran as fast as her legs would carry her through the forest and towards her cottage. She hoped her mother was inside, and was glad to find her preparing food.

"Mother, mother," Ivy gasped, barely able to get the words out for shortness of breath.

"Slow down, Ivy, slow down," said her mother. "Take a deep breath and slow down."

Ivy sank onto a chair and after taking two deep breaths said, "There's a man in the forest, a black robe and he's really badly hurt, mother. What shall we do?"

Elspeth looked both surprised and alarmed and asked. "Who is he? Have you any idea?"

"Well, actually, I'm sorry I didn't tell you earlier mother, but I did see the same man in the forest this morning," said Ivy.

"Ivy, this is very serious. These people are becoming our enemies. We must be very careful what we do and say around them. Did he ask you anything or tell you anything?"

Ivy felt like she might be in trouble if she told her mother the truth, that she actually had said something to the man, so she decided to tell her part of the truth. "He asked me what we did by the river and just now he told me he was badly hurt. Mother we must help him."

Ivy did not quite know why she said this, as after all weren't these people their sworn enemies? She just felt in her bones that the man must be helped.

"Alright, Ivy," said Elspeth. "The choice to me is clear. We must go and see what we can do. Let me get my medicine bag and a selection of herbs and ointments."

In a few minutes Ivy and her mother were on their way to the big rock. Elspeth stopped briefly at the gathering on the heath to tell her friend Marlea that she and Ivy would be going to the forest and that they would be back in twenty minutes. Elspeth thought this was necessary in case they met with any trouble. As they approached the rock, Ivy noticed that her mother's hand moved down to rest on the hilt of the little dagger that she wore on her belt. The forest was silent, but the man was still there.

Elspeth and Ivy crept slowly and cautiously towards the body that was collapsed below the rock. Ivy began to wonder if the man was even still alive. But as they approached they heard a groan and a spluttering cough as the man struggled to catch his breath. Suddenly Elspeth spoke with a gentle but commanding tone, "We have come to assist you. Do not move or struggle." The man seemed to hear and slowly turned his head towards them. Elspeth unfastened the pouch from her belt

27

and knelt down to examine the man's wounds. He had a huge gash on his forehead and his leg was twisted back in such a way that it must have been broken. He seemed to struggle in and out of consciousness, and moaned softly as if in great pain. After running her hand a few inches above and around his body, Elspeth spoke. "He is too hurt to move," she said to Ivy. "We must get the carrier from Tamar and have him brought to the house so that his wounds can be properly tended. I will go and alert Tamar. You can return to the festivities Ivy. I do not want you to miss any more fun. It's alright. The man is so badly wounded he's not dangerous. And when he's recovered we can post a guard near him if necessary. Tell Marlea that all is well, but ask her to come to Tamar's. We shall need her healing powers to help this man."

Ivy and Elspeth parted company as Elspeth hurried to Tamar's cottage to get help carrying the man. Ivy returned to the heath where the villagers were still playing games and merrily sharing their day of fun and celebration. The thunderheads in the east had dispersed and all seemed well as the summer sun shone down on the festivities. Ivy wondered if the man with the silver cross had been sent to spy on the village and would then report his findings to the priest on the stallion, who would then decide whether to attack the village or not. The injury of the young man would prevent such a report from going through, which would be good for the villagers. But how would the priests react when their young spy did not return? That was a troubling thought.

It was soon time for the big feast of the day and tables and chairs were being arranged so that the food could be brought out. Soon wonderful smells filled the air as pies and soups and other delicious foods were arranged on the long tables. Pitchers of water and cider from last year's pressing were being brought out and vases full of brilliantly colored flowers were being set on the table too. Ivy went to the cottage and fetched the bread that her mother had baked that morning. She was beginning to wonder how long her mother was going to take attending the man with the silver cross, when suddenly there was Elspeth with a group of other women. Ivy looked questioningly at her mother.

"Everything is under control, Ivy," said Elspeth, as if reading her daughter's mind. "We have tended to the wounds of the young priest. He is asleep and still cannot talk coherently, and it will be a while before he will be able to walk. It is an interesting turn of events. We will see what having a black robe in our midst does for the situation. This could make things very interesting."

"I hope it does more good than harm, mother," said Ivy. "What will the priests do when he does not return?"

"We shall have to wait and see, Ivy," said her mother. "But something tells me that this event will end up serving us, not harming us. Now let us go and enjoy the feast. There's no more we can do now. At sunset Tamar has asked the women to gather to perform a very sacred and urgent ritual for this time. I want you to be there, Ivy. And I want you to pay special attention. I want you to learn from these times, so that when your time comes you will be prepared and can use what you have learned." With a mixture of delight and apprehension at her mother's words, Ivy sat down to eat.

7

As the sun began dipping towards the horizon, the villagers finished their feast and began clearing away their dishes, pots and bowls to prepare for the setting sun rituals. Each group in the village met and performed a ritual for the continuance and sustenance of their village and their livelihoods. There was the mill workers' group, those folks who ground the grain and made the flour for the village. They met in a circle and asked for the ripeness of the grain and the success of its harvest. Then there was the farmers' group, that most central and essential group of villagers who tended the crops. Over by the spreading oak tree was the blacksmiths' circle, those folk who forged metal and shoed the horses. As the separate groups began to gather, Ivy and her mother went into the forest to meet with the group of women who were the healers and enchanterers of the village. Tamar was there to meet them.

The group gathered round as Tamar began to speak. "Friends and wise ones, we meet today as we have never met before. A new wind is blowing, one that we neither know nor understand. Today an event happened that is the turning point that I had seen coming. A man now resides with us, a stranger." A murmur of fear and questions trembled through the group of women. Tamar spoke on. "He is a black robe, and he is badly injured. Elspeth and her daughter Ivy brought him to my forest house just a little while ago. They found him injured in the forest. He had fallen from a rock whilst spying on our river bower rituals. The rock's energy has protected us, wise ones," she said with a smile. "The ritual of the stones this morning worked its magic quickly, dear ones. Your magic is powerful. The man was not able to return to his masters to report on our doings in the sacred bower. Now we have him in our midst. But we must do more. Ivy, since it was you who discovered this man, this spy, I see that as a sign of your growing power. It is you I choose to light the fire. Prepare yourself little one. Here is the lighter stick."

Tamar unwrapped from a purple cloth that was decorated with a dragon design, a thick fir branch that had been carved at one end with magical symbols and letters. She then stooped down and pulled from her pocket a flint and tinder box. As she worked, the drill spun in the socket, and smoke started to rise from the dried grasses beneath the tinder. Soon a glowing flame appeared and the grasses caught fire. She put small sticks and branches on the fire so that a small blaze erupted. Soon the kindling was hot enough to light the special lighter stick. All the time that Tamar worked she sang a low soft chant and would sometimes stop and close her eyes in concentration. When the lighter stick was glowing red, Tamar held it with two hands and raised it slowly over her head and then back down to the ground again.

Then she spoke, "Ivy. As the representative of the goddess, I ask that you light the sacred fire of the forest. Go now, and we shall follow." Ivy placed her hands reverentially around the base of the exquisitely carved stick and started to walk slowly towards the clearing in the forest where the women gathered for seasonal rituals. As she trod through the forest, she felt a chant rise up through the earth, the stick, the sky, the trees. It was a chant that she did not know until this moment and it was in a language unlike her own. With the chant pounding inside her, repeating it over and over, she reached the fire circle and knelt down beside the already prepared kindling and felt herself move into a trance-like state, as a prayer formed on her lips. She took a couple of cleansing breaths and then the prayer began to spill from within her.

"Great mother, divine spirits, I pray for the continuance of life, of clarity in times of strife, of your blessing on the work we do, and your guidance in these days ahead." She bowed her head and flames danced in the fire she had started. She turned and handed the lighter stick back to Tamar, and at once felt the spirit leave her and her breath soften as the stick left her hands. The women had gathered around her in the clearing and encircled the fire. It was time to begin. The light was lit. The circle cast.

8

The villagers left their groups as the sunset rituals were complete, and headed for the heath. Some returned to their cottages to rest, and some gathered around a large bonfire that had been lit in the field. There was a feeling of relief in the air. The villagers had successfully completed their day of solstice celebrations without being troubled by the black robes. Much of the talk around the fire was about the young black robe that Ivy had found injured by the stream. There was a lot of discussion about him and what he was up to in the forest. Other groups of villagers picked up their instruments and played some merry tunes.

The women's circle in the forest was complete, too, and Ivy and Elspeth made their way back to their cottage weary from the day's events, but a warm sensation of peace and accomplishment accompanied their tiredness.

"What will we do with the young man, mother?" asked Ivy as she and her mother sat next to the fire, drinking a soothing cup of chamomile tea before going to bed. "Is it safe to keep him here in the village?"

"I expect we'll nurse him back to health and then he'll be gone. Some may want to keep him captive as a hostage, but I suspect that we'll not want to bring any more of the black robes' wrath down on the village and will let him go peacefully. Maybe his stay with us will help him understand us a little better and he'll go and tell his friends to leave us in peace. We are certainly not harming anyone with our ways. I wonder what makes those men so determined to change us. Why can't we all live together in peace?"

And with that question on their minds, Ivy and Elspeth went to sleep for the night. As Ivy lay in her bed, sleep evaded her for a while, and she watched the beautiful sliver of a new moon rise outside her window. As the moon rose she thought of the events of the day, how she had spoken to the young black robe, how he had been gentle of manner, and how she had later found him wounded and unconscious. And she also thought of the great rituals at the stone circle and then later in the forest. Her heart glowed with pride at the memory of being acclaimed by Tamar, and the honor that it was to light the fire stick for the sunset ceremony. Now her thoughts spread to the future and how she was to train with the other priestesses and learn more of the ancient ways. She was becoming a part of the ancient circle, a circle that stretched far into the distant past, and, she hoped, way into the future. "If the black robes don't stop it," she thought.

As the day softly slipped from her mind and sleep embraced her, another voice whispered in her mind. It was the mysterious voice that she had heard by the river. "Speak, write and all will be told. Speak, write and all will be told....."

9

As the young black robe's eyes tried to come into focus the next morning, he found that his sight was very hazy and that his head hurt so much he thought he was going to lose consciousness again. He could feel intense pain in his right leg and ribs. With alarm he realized what had happened to him and that here he lay in a strange room full of very unusual smells and sights. His heart skipped a beat as he realized further that he was in Stoneleigh, in the home of one of the villagers. He heard a cock crow and had to close his eyes again as they hurt so much. The sound of an old woman's voice outside made him freeze with fear.

"There Shadow, my wise one, up you go, up into your basket." It was Tamar and her cat. "Wishy, wishy, splishy, splashy. Make my potion strong, " she intoned as she stirred a new batch of healing tea. The young man felt a strong pressure of fear bear down on his chest. His breath quickened. He was in the home of a witch!

The young man had been named Luke, after one of Jesus Christ's followers, and had been ordained into the priesthood

37

very recently, during the last autumn. But he had heard tell of the ways of villagers in remote places like Stoneleigh who had not yet converted to the Christian faith. Luke had been raised in a Christian household in the south and had been sworn into the priesthood when he was still a young lad. He had come to help spread the Christian ways into the northlands with some fellow priests from the abbey of Tincallon. They had taught him about witches and their craft. They said it was known that witches brewed evil spells and used black magic in consort with the fallen angels. They also told him that they sacrificed animals and small children at their altars in the forest and in their strange stone circles. Luke had even witnessed the destruction of one heathen circle at Wincomb, when the priests had instructed some of the Christian lords to destroy the circle because it was a place where people gathered to worship the devil. The lords and some of their followers had gathered one night and taken battering rams and ropes and pulleys and knocked down the giant stone circle, as the gleeful priests looked on. Luke was now paralyzed with fear. Here he was, in the camp of the enemy. What would they do with him, sacrifice him to the devil?

He heard Tamar shuffling around outside and wondered what evil brew she was concocting. Looking around, Luke could see plants and animal skins hanging from the rafters and all over the table were jars and bottles of different colored evil-looking liquids. What should he do? As the door to the cottage opened he decided it would be best for him to feign sleep, so he lay back still and quiet.

"Arr, the young black robe still sleeps, Shadow," said Tamar to her cat who had followed her inside. "I must change the compress on his leg, and give him a new one. That leg is in bad condition. Bad. Very bad." With that she bent down to remove a bundle of soaked cloth from the young man's leg. Luke could stay still no more, and opened his eyes in horror of the old, wizened woman touching him.

"Get back," he cried, and grabbed for the silver cross around his neck. Somehow he felt that it could protect him.

Tamar chuckled and said, "I'm not going to harm you, young fellow. Your leg will fester if you don't get help. You're not going anywhere you know. That leg is broken as well as cut. Elspeth will be over in a while to put a splint to it. You'll be with us a while, so don't be afraid. We do not seek to harm you, stranger though you be. Why are you in these parts?"

Luke was taken aback. This old woman seemed kindly, rather like his old grandmother or his nurse Gertrude, not like an evil witch who would spit venom and darkness. But he'd better be careful. She was probably good at deceit and deception.

"I thank you, but I must return to my friends. They will be concerned as to my whereabouts," he spoke in a faltering way, his voice crackling in pain. "Would one of your people take a message down to the little church in the valley and tell them where to find me?"

But Tamar just smiled and said, "All in good time, my boy. All in good time." And with that she bent down to dress his wound. He knew he had neither the strength to struggle nor the ability to get up and run, as the pain was so great in his leg. So, with a sigh, he sank back onto his pillow. He kept one hand on his silver cross and the other felt across to his pocket. He heaved a sigh of relief. There was his holy book safe in his pocket. He put his other hand securely around it. At least he had his bible, his holy book. That would bring him comfort.

10

Ivy and Elspeth had risen early the morning after the solstice and had gone about their normal morning ritual for the new day. The return of the sun and the giving of thanks for the new day was celebrated in all the village homes. Ivy and Elspeth usually lit one of their home-made beeswax candles and said a short prayer, facing the east, the direction of the new morning sun as it rose over the forest. Then they started to prepare for the day ahead. Ivy reflected on the events of the day before and what a powerful day it had been for her. She and Elspeth were planning to go and visit Tamar and the young priest that morning so that Elspeth could set a splint to the young man's broken leg. Elspeth had instructed Ivy in the plants that they would need to be gathered to apply to the priest's wounds to help in his healing, and now Ivy was out in the forest gathering plants.

She had been taught to identify and gather medicinal plants from a very early age and recognized most of the common ones that were used by her mother and the other healers of the village. Now she knew that she would be taught the blessings and prayers that went along with these plants in their application. Her mother had always told her that the gift of medicinal plants was sacred, and one must treat them with immense respect, and always give thanks when picking them for use. Then their healing properties were much more likely to be effective. The healers also knew special incantations that they either spoke out loud or muttered quietly as they used their medicine. This also gave added special healing properties to their work. Ivy was excited to think that she was beginning her apprenticeship with her mother in these most treasured healing arts.

As she gathered medicinal plants from the forest she tried to focus her mind on the healing needed by the young black robe and also the wish that he could begin to see her people's true nature, not as enemies but as friends. When her basket was full, she headed back to the cottage and she and her mother set out for Tamar's forest dwelling.

When Elspeth and Ivy arrived at Tamar's, the old woman was sitting outside in the dappled morning light, shredding comfrey leaves into a wooden bowl.

"Oh, Elspeth, Ivy, I am pleased you are here so early. The young man's leg must be attended to as the bone must be aligned. Let us go inside and see to it immediately," said Tamar.

The young priest, Luke, was lying still with his eyes closed, his whole body still throbbing with pain. He heard

42

someone come in and slowly blinked open his eyes. He recognized Ivy, the young girl he had seen at the riverside, and then again by the big rock where he had taken his fall.

"Young man," said Elspeth. "We have come to set your leg in a splint. It is badly broken. So lie still, we will be gentle. First drink this tea I have brewed fresh this morning. It will soothe you so that you can relax."

Luke was immediately suspicious. He wondered what kind of evil brew she wanted to feed him. It would probably make him sicker or maybe even poison him.

"I do not want you to touch me nor do I want to drink that stuff," he said angrily. "My only wish is that you tell my people where I am, so that they can come and fetch me. They will tend to my wounds."

"My dear boy, " said Tamar. "You are far too wounded to be moved. Your leg must heal before you can go anywhere. Now lie back and don't worry. We are experts in the healing ways. We will make sure you are set right. Now drink the tea. It will calm you."

Luke lay back with a sigh. It was true. He could not run or escape from this evil-smelling place. He had no choice but to pray to his god for safety and hope that these women knew what they were doing. He cautiously took a few sips of the tea that Elspeth offered him and soon felt a little easier. The tea was delicious and soothing, so he drank a little more. Elspeth started

43

her work, with Ivy in assistance, handing her tools and herbal mixtures that she placed on the man's wounds.

Elspeth set the splint and applied the ointments and salves. After a while, Elspeth said to Tamar, "Come, we must speak. Let us step outside. Ivy, stay here and see that the young man does well with our medicine. We shall be outside if you need us."

"Alright, mother, as you wish," Ivy said as she sat on a stool next to the man's bed. She was a little afraid of him, and made sure that she sat out of arm's reach. But she knew that he would not be able to get up.

Luke was feeling a lot better. The pains were starting to subside and he felt more relaxed. The women had been very gentle in their treatment of him and the herbal brews they had given him were pleasant-tasting and did indeed seem to relax him.

"My name is Luke, young one. May I ask yours?" he said softly.

Ivy's voice faltered, but she told him her name.

"I have to thank you for helping me when I fell from the rock. I could be lying there still if it had not been for you," said the young man.

Ivy felt some anger stir within her. He was, after all, a spy sent to gather information about her people that could well put them in danger. She lowered her eyes, and would not talk to him. Her eyes came to rest on a book that was lying under the

44

man's arm. It was his bible, the holy book of the Christians. Ivy was fascinated. She had never seen a book before. No one in the village knew how to read. The lord of the manor knew how to read and write, but the people of the villages never had access to that knowledge. She was very curious about this book that lay next to the priest. Should she ask if she could look at it? A strong voice from within told her that this was the thing to do.

"I am pleased that you are comfortable," she said slowly to him. "May I ask what is in that book you have there?" she asked nodding towards the book.

Luke saw this as an opportunity to tell this young woman a little about the life of Christ. He had been trained in how to convert pagans away from their beliefs in nature spirits and other devilish ideas, and to bring them into the awareness of the one and only true god and his son Jesus Christ.

"This, my child, is what we call a bible. It contains the teachings of our savior, Jesus Christ. Do you know of what I speak?" he said.

Ivy replied, "I have heard his name before. But what I know of his teachings is that he tells people that our ways are evil. We are not bad people, so I care not for this Christ. But I would care to understand more. Could I see your book? I cannot read, but would like to look at it."

Luke did not want Ivy to touch his bible, being afraid that she would run off with it or throw it into the fire. But he saw no harm in showing her the pages while he held it tightly.

"Here, Ivy. These are the words of Christ and the teaching of his followers," he said and opened the book up reverentially so that Ivy could see a few pages. "They speak of love and salvation. Christ offers eternal peace to all who follow his ways."

Ivy stared at the black shapes that were laid out in lines across the page. This book had been written by hand and was covered in these inky scratches.

"Each mark is a sound, and each group of marks is a word. When you know the meaning of each mark you can read what is being said. I myself wrote this book. I copied each letter and each word from the bible at the monastery where I live. It took me a whole year to do. I worked on it every day. I was glad to do this work as now I have a bible I can carry with me wherever I go." He turned the pages slowly so that Ivy could see his work. She thought it astonishingly beautiful, and wished she knew what it said.

"Could you, would you, read me a little? I mean, I would really love to hear what is being said in these pages," asked Ivy.

Luke was delighted. Here was a chance to teach this young ignorant village girl about the teachings of Jesus of Nazareth. Maybe he could work his way into the hearts and minds of these simple people.

"I would be pleased to read to you, Ivy," and he opened up the book. "In the beginning ..."

He had read but three words when the door opened and in walked Elspeth. Luke lay down his book and slipped it under the covers, thinking that this witch might not approve of his reading from the bible to her daughter. She might even seize it from him.

"Come, Ivy. We must go now," said Elspeth to her daughter. "This man needs rest and we have work to do."

Ivy was disappointed. She wanted to hear more of the book, but had to go with her mother.

"I thank you for your kindness," said Luke to Elspeth. "Come back soon will you, and bring young Ivy. We were enjoying one another's company. We will share more later on, Ivy, yes?"

"We shall return later with some fresh herbs," said Elspeth. "Tamar will give you the rest of what we brought today. Be sure to take what she offers you, for it will speed the healing." And with that Ivy and Elspeth left, and Luke closed his eyes to sleep.

11

When Ivy and her mother returned from their work at Tamar's forest house, there was a group of villagers awaiting their arrival at the cottage.

"How does the young man this morning, Elspeth?" asked her friend Marlea.

"His bone is set and the wounds dressed. He is still in great pain. But he will survive," answered Elspeth.

"While you were gone, we had a meeting, Elspeth," said Jack the miller. "We have decided to keep the boy hostage, and if the priests continue to harass us we can threaten his life to keep them at bay. He must remain well-hidden, so that if the priests come sniffing around they won't find him. What is your opinion?"

"I think it a good solution, friends. But the young man will soon need a guard, as he will have movement in a couple of days when the pain subsides and the leg begins its healing."

"We have a group of people who have agreed to take turns guarding him," said Marlea.

"Then, so be it," answered Elspeth. "Why here comes that black robe now." She pointed to the horizon where a man on a horse could been seen approaching at a gallop with another at his side.

Other villagers came out of their cottages to stand firm against the priest. Some carried sticks and hoes. Others stayed hidden where they could observe the meeting in secret.

The man in the black robe had a thin, tired face that was ruddied from the ride. He was breathless when he pulled up in front of the group of villagers, and the man that rode beside him was the first to speak.

"I am John, the representative of his lordship of Stoneleigh. This Christian priest has reported that one of his young brethren came this way yester morn, and has not returned. What say you? Has anyone seen this man? His name is Luke."

"No one of that name has been seen here. But this man," said Jack the miller pointing at the old black robe, "he was here yesterday and he threatened us. His manner was very disturbing. We ask that you tell his lordship to inform the priests to leave us be. They have no right bothering us. We will leave them alone if they will leave us alone."

"Now, friends, " said John. "The priests bring the word of God Almighty to our lands. We welcome them. His lordship just gave a handsome sum to Brother Pius here to finish the building of their church down in the valley. We must treat them as guests. His lordship has welcomed them."

"Then they should also extend a hand of friendship towards us," said Elspeth. "Instead they mock our ways and threaten to destroy our holy places. We wish to be left in peace." She paused. "If we do see this missing young man we will treat him with due courtesy, so long as we receive the same from him."

John looked a little annoyed, but the red-faced priest could not keep himself from blurting out, "Come to Christ. He is the Savior. There is only one true God. The kingdom of heaven awaits you. Repent!"

The villagers smiled and looked a little amused at this man's ravings.

"Peace be with *you*," said Elspeth as the villagers turned towards their homes. The pair on horseback rode away, not fully satisfied with what they had heard.

12

Ivy and Elspeth returned to their cottage to begin their day's chores. "My dear daughter," said Elspeth. "Today we will work on the dyeing of the wool to make your very own cloak of power. We shall weave magic into it, so that it will keep you strong and safe. While we work we shall talk of the many rituals used here and how they protect us and our lands. Take down the reed basket from the loft. In it are the plants we shall need for the dye."

Ivy unpacked the reed basket and found many packets of different dried plants, roots and fungi. She recognized a few of them, but many were unfamiliar and she expected that they came from other regions. Elspeth filled her cauldron with water and started to add plants to the mix. As each one was placed in the steaming kettle she told Ivy its name and where it could be gathered. She also repeated an incantation, a spell that was to be woven in with the magic of the plants. The water in the pot soon started to turn a beautiful shade of purple. It was then time to add the woven fabric. As this was done another blessing was repeated as the mixture was completely stirred. Elspeth and Ivy took turns in stirring the mixture so that the dye would completely penetrate the cloth. The pale yellowish fabric started to turn into a gorgeous amethyst purple. It had the shine and shimmer of the amethyst gems that Ivy had seen inlaid in her mother's staff. As Ivy stirred she sang and chanted and her heart was filled with the pleasure and power of the moment. She was becoming a healer and priestess like her mother.

When the cauldron had been stirred for many hours it was time to remove the cloth. Ivy helped her mother pour off the liquid and then hang the cloth up to dry in the afternoon sun. Ivy had learnt such a lot today, how to make a special dye, how to give it power, and many other things that Elspeth had shared with her about the uses of the cloak and the times it could be used.

By mid afternoon Elspeth said, "It's time now to change the poultice on the young man's wounds. Ivy I would like you to run to Tamar's with the fresh herbs she'll need and assist her. I must go and talk to our neighbors about what we shall do if that priest returns or if the lord sends his men to look for Luke. Run along now, but be careful in case anyone is already snooping around."

Ivy ran through the forest carrying the bundle of herbs. It took her a while to reach Tamar's, but she saw nobody else on the way. Tamar was glad to see her and at once they set to work.

Luke was sitting upright in bed and was reading his book when Ivy walked in. Shadow the cat had appeared to have befriended the young man, because there he sat at Luke's feet.

"Hello, Ivy," said the priest with a smile. "Your medicine is working miracles. I am feeling so much better." Luke hated to admit this, but it was becoming clearer to him that the ways of these simple peasants were not evil in the way he had been told, and that their remedies did seem to work.

"I am pleased to hear of that, sir," said Ivy, politely. "I bring fresh plants for your wounds. Shall I tend to him, grandmother?" she asked Tamar. Tamar nodded and said that she had wood to chop in the forest and would return after a while.

Ivy had her reasons for wanting to help. She had been fascinated by his book and the writings therein and wanted to see more. After she had put fresh poultices on his leg and head, Ivy felt the strength rise in her to ask if she could see the book.

"Why of course, Ivy," said Luke, thinking that he could teach Ivy more about the teachings of Christ and this was what was spurring her interest. "Here you are. You may look at it yourself, and then I will read some more to you."

He handed her the book, feeling that he could now trust her. Ivy took it carefully into her hands and then opened it up to take a close look at the inky marks inside. She could see that each line had a group of marks strung across it. Some groups had only one mark. Some had as many as six or seven. Luke had told her that morning that each mark represented a sound. What were those sounds? She remembered the three words that Luke had read to her that morning, "In the beginning ....." So she looked at the first groups of marks on the first page. She tried to match the words with the marks she saw on the page. As she stared at the words a shiver ran through her body and a cloud seemed to pass over her eyes. She felt as though she was sinking into a trance. The words on the page suddenly became very sharp and clear and seemed to almost burn into her consciousness. "In the beginning..." she repeated over and over to herself. Luke began to get a little worried and wondered why she was staring so intently at the page. Was there some evil magic going on?

"Ivy, let me read on," he said, thinking that the words of Christ would chase out any demons, should they be lurking. He took the book from her and continued to read. After a few lines, Ivy heard herself interrupt him.

"Please tell me what each mark represents so that I may read these beautiful words for myself," she asked. Luke was pleased. Obviously the words of God were so powerful that Ivy wanted to be able to read them herself.

"Well, little one. It goes like this. The 'marks' as you call them are letters. The letters are known as the alphabet. There are 26 letters in the alphabet. Each letter has a sound." And he told Ivy what the letters of the alphabet were. "So," he went on, " the first word here is 'in'. That is made with the sound 'i' and 'n'. In. Here, fetch me a charcoal stick from the fire. I will write out the letters of the alphabet for you."

And so, on a thin piece of wood that Ivy found by the fire, Luke wrote out the letters of the alphabet, repeating the sound of each letter as he wrote. Ivy felt her mind grow sharp and focused again as he did this. This knowledge seemed to penetrate deep into her being.

"Now, Ivy, let me read more to you from the holy book," said Luke. But Ivy could not listen to the words he read, she stared at the marks on the wood. Yes! she would learn to read! She carefully slipped the piece of wood into her basket and covered it with a cloth, and then prepared to leave.

"I shall return tomorrow, " she told the young priest. "Can we read more then?"

"Of course. It will be my pleasure. But I expect to be gone any time now, Ivy. I just know my people will be looking for me."

With that troubling thought, Ivy left Tamar's cottage. As she stepped onto the path home she ran into Jeb, one of the village carpenters. He was carrying a big stick and had his long knife in his belt.

"I am come to guard that sniveling priest, young one. Now, run along," he said gruffly as Ivy hurried past him. The sounds were pounding in her head, "A. B. C ..."

13

When Ivy lay down in her bed that night she had many thoughts on her mind before sleep would come. There were the lessons of her mother who had taught her so much on this day of the workings of a wise woman and priestess. Then there were the words of the young priest and how she had learned of the alphabet and the first steps of reading and writing. As sleep began to overwhelm her, the words that she had heard by the riverside returned. "Speak, write and all will be told. Speak, write and all will be told..." As Ivy lay in that place that is half way between awakening and sleep, her mind drifted to the scene of a young woman who was sitting beneath a mighty, ancient oak tree. All around her were the glimmers of light that are the fairy folk. They hovered and danced in the dappled sunlight, their tiny rainbow wings flashing and fluttering. Some hovered by the young woman's side. Others whispered secrets in her ear. The young woman had a book on her lap and a quill pen in her hand. As Ivy's mind drifted into focus, she realized with a start that the young woman was herself, and she was writing, writing something down. Ivy was thrilled at the thought that she may be seeing into the future, and that one day she would indeed be able to write. Then the book came into focus. It was a leather-bound text with inky scratches on its pages. Ivy then saw what those inky scratches were. They were the words of wisdom that she was now learning from her mother. The words from the river spirit then came again, "Speak, write and all will be told....." and suddenly it all became very clear to Ivy. It was as though the sun had just come out from behind the clouds. She was to learn to record the wisdom of her people! She would write down the rituals and the remedies, the names of the plants that heal and the spells to cast. She would write it all down so that it would last forever. That was it. She would write down the sacred knowledge of her people! The teachings of Luke of how to read and write would be put to good use. She would document the teachings of her mother and the other wise women. The sacred knowledge would never be lost. Her writings could stretch far into the future, so that others might read them. The images began to fade from her mind. The fairy light grew dim and the blanket of sleep engulfed her.

For the next seven and twenty days Ivy spent her time with Luke, helping him to heal his wounds and learning more and more of the skills of reading and writing. He wrote down words for her to take home and practice reading and writing over and over, so that she got the idea of how the letters joined made words. At the same time, Ivy's mother was teaching her about the medicinal plants, what spells to use for different needs and more and more about the ancient rituals of her people. Ivy felt like a vessel into which was being poured a rich healing potion. She was now writing her first words, and practising late into the night to remember the sounds of the letters and the names of the plants and the secret chants of her people.

Luke's head priest had visited again during this time and asked more questions and gone away irritated and upset. The villagers knew that it was only a matter of time before more serious trouble would arrive on their doorstep. They kept a watch through the night and made sure that Luke, who could now walk a little bit, was prevented from leaving.

On the eight and twentieth night since Luke had stumbled into their midst, the villagers were awakened by shrieks and screams and the heavy sound of horses racing through the village. Ivy opened her eyes to find that the windows of the cottage were glowing a hot red. Something was on fire! She stumbled out into the darkness, her heart pounding, to see masked horsemen with flaming torches, galloping through the streets. One thatched roof cottage was already on fire. Flames were leaping and licking across the tinder-dry roof of Jan the carpenter's house. Jan and his family were rushing out of their house with some of their possessions, while others formed a line to pass water buckets from the river to try and dowse the fire. Another fire sprang to life in the distance. It looked as though the dark riders had set fire to a hay rick in Farmer Gray's field. Then Ivy saw them turn and ride back towards the center of the town. They halted as an angry mob descended on them. One of the horsemen shouted, "We will longer tolerate your blasphemy, people of Stoneleigh. Return our young priest or we shall be back tomorrow with more men and greater weapons. We know that you conceal him here. You are warned!" A fight ensued. While Ivy and Elspeth ran to help with the dowsing of the fires, other villagers tried to wrestle the horsemen to the ground. But the horsemen were stronger and had longer knives that flashed and cut, and several villagers fell shrieking to the ground, crying in pain from the wounds made by the dark riders. The men on horseback shouted a retreat and sped off across the moors, while the people were left to tend to the wounded and watch the remains of Jan's house burn to the ground.

Dawn was starting to appear in the sky when the people finally returned, exhausted, to their cottages. Ivy and her mother sat by the embers of their hearth fire and sipped some tea. "What should we do, mother?" asked Ivy. But the reply never came. There was a heavy pounding on the front door. Elspeth rose to open it. There stood the bailiff from the nearby market town. Behind him flamed the pink new morning sky. "I have a warrant for the arrest of Elspeth Yarrow," his deep voice boomed. "The charge is witchcraft!" Two burly men strode into the cottage, seized Elspeth roughly by the arms and dragged her out to a waiting cart. She struggled and cursed them under her breath, but was soon tied at the wrist. As one of the men stooped down to tie a gag around her mouth Elspeth screamed out to Ivy. "You know what to do. Be brave my daughter..." She was then muffled to silence.

Ivy was in shock. Her mother arrested as a witch! What did this all mean? She ran to Marlea's house and told her what had happened. "Alas," spoke Marlea, "the plague has arrived. We have heard tell of this type of thing happening in the southlands. We never dreamt that this pestilence would spread here. They want to call the wise women 'witches'. They say our healing is dangerous and our spells and incantations are the work of an evil force that they call the devil. They are threatened by our knowledge because it weakens theirs. The morning grows light but a darkness is spreading through this land. They say that this is the teaching of a holy man who wanted peace on earth, goodwill to all men. But these priests are bringing death to the land, and war. Ivy, we must stay strong in our hearts. Come little one. Come sit with me, we must summon up all the powers we know to protect your mother."

Ivy stumbled into Marlea's house as Marlea took down her cloak of power and her sacred staff. Ivy knew the spell of protection. It was one of the ones she had learned just that week. She closed her eyes and focused all her thoughts on the healing words. She pictured a cloak of courage surrounding her mother. After they had finished their work Ivy collapsed onto Marlea's lap and wept. Her mother was gone.

14

A group of villagers gathered in Marlea's cottage later that morning. They discussed what to do. Some felt that the young priest, Luke, could tell the bailiff to release Elspeth, for surely he knew that Elspeth was not an evil witch but a wise woman and healer, for had she not healed his wounds? Others thought they should arrange for a trade: Luke's freedom for Elspeth's. Many thought that those associated with the priests could not be trusted, and so extreme caution must be exercised. It was finally decided to go once more to seek Tamar's advice, for she knew Luke better than any of them. Sam the potter came in and said that he had been in town collecting supplies when he saw a cart heading for the jail. In it were four or five women, amongst them was Elspeth. "All accused of witchcraft?" Marlea asked. Sam knodded his head with a heavy sigh. Marlea said she would travel into town that afternoon with a few of her fellow villagers to see if anything could be done and to bring some clothes and food to Elspeth.

Ivy begged, "Please let me come too. I won't be any trouble. I must see my mother!"

"Girl, it is dangerous. You'd best stay at home," was the reply she received. But Ivy would not hear of it, and the villagers finally agreed to take her along. Ivy went to her cottage to gather some things to take to her mother. She packed a basket with some freshly baked bread, a hunk of cheese and some dried apples from last year's harvest, but then started to wonder what she could pack her mother that would come in even more useful. "Yes," she realized, "her cloak! The guards at the prison will not dream it to be anything but an old moth-eaten cloak. Surely they'll let me give it to her for warmth! And I can hide some herbs within it. If she has her cloak, she will be invincible!" Ivy prepared pouches of herbs to hide in the cloak. And lastly she picked up her mother's little dagger and strapped it to her belt, concealing it with her own cloak.

Marlea and Ivy had arrived in town after several hours of riding across difficult terrain. The village of Stoneleigh was isolated from the outside world. Ivy had only been to the town twice in her life before and was amazed at the number of people there and all the hustle and bustle of activity. There were people carrying cages of chickens to market, musicians performing on street corners, and horses and carts jamming up the roads as people made their way through the windy streets. Then Ivy's attention fell on some signs that were posted on a wall near the market place. It suddenly dawned on her that she might be able to read these signs. She was thrilled at the possibility. She came up close to the sign and sounded out each letter of each word and then tried to string them together to make some kind of sense.

"For the crime of witchcraft," the sign read, "death by hanging." And below there was a list of names, "Mary Talbot, Irene Reed, Frances Jenkins, April Smith..." Ivy's heart skipped a beat, for the last name in the list was her mother's, Elspeth Yarrow. Ivy's head swam with the words that she had read from the sign. Her mother to hang as a witch? The thought was too horrifying to be true. Ivy's mind switched from disbelief, to anger and then to action. She must get to the prison, and she had to get her mother out. She ran to catch up with the others and tell them the awful news.

Marlea spoke, "The tide of evil grows fast upon this land. We must try to turn this tragedy around. Do the people not see what is going on? These Christians do not teach the words of Christ. They work from greed and ambition. Soon the ancient ways will be lost in a flood of their outrage. Did not I hear tell that Christ taught that it was wrong to commit murder? So what is the hanging of innocent women but wholesale murder? Oh my, what is going to become of us?"

She sank her head in her hands in desperation for a moment, then lifted her head with a proud shake, and a look of power and defiance flashed in her eyes. "But we are not defeated yet. Let's make a plan." The group found a spot in the shade of an oak tree and figured out what to do next. They joined hands and began to breathe deeply, drawing power from the rich earth, the oak tree and the air. It was their way of strengthening and calming their minds for decision. After a lot of discussion and careful planning they were ready for action.

"We shall not go down without a fight!" Marlea said and strode towards the prison gate, Ivy hurrying to catch up with her.

When Marlea, Ivy and the others reached the prison gates, they found a guard stationed at the door. Marlea spoke up at once. "My friend has been detained, kind sir," said Marlea in the most ingratiating tone she could muster. "We have brought her a little to eat and some extra besides." She pulled out a bottle of apple cider from the basket, knowing that the prison guard was probably pretty easy to bribe.

He said, "Let's see what you have in that there basket, " and roughly searched the contents. "I can see nothing amiss. But I'll take this and this." He removed the apples and cheese from the basket. "The bread'll do 'em," he snarled. "It looks pretty wormy."

"We also brought the woman Elspeth's old cloak for warmth. She was taken before she could get properly dressed," said Marlea. The man snarled and turned his nose up at the old cloak, thinking that what he smelt was dampness and dust, not the herbal pouches that Ivy had sewn into the seams. He then took a long draft of the apple cider and instantly his manner mellowed and he grabbed the cloak. With that he curled his lip and bared his rotten black teeth, and took the basket into the prison, slamming the door behind him. Ivy smiled to herself. The magic had worked and the man had carried into her mother the tools it would take to break her free. Ivy breathed a deep sigh of relief.

15

The women returned to the village. Ivy had hoped to stay closer to town so that she would be nearer her mother, but Marlea thought it far too dangerous. When they arrived home, Ivy went despondently to her cottage, feeling a chill as she walked into an empty home. Her mother's absence rang like a hollow note. Ivy sank onto her bed and slept and slept. No dreams visited her that night.

When she awoke it was many hours later, and was starting to turn dark. The silver glow of the moon rising shone through her window, and she wondered what her mother was doing in her prison cell. Ivy got up and suddenly thought of the young priest, Luke. What had become of him since the arrests? She decided she must find out for herself. And what of Tamar? Was she safe? As the wisest woman of the village, surely Tamar was in danger too.

Ivy moved as quietly and stealthily as a fox through the forest as her mother had taught her to do. The moon helped light her way, but she knew the path well. She felt comforted being in the forest again, and even thought she saw a twinkle in the grass that was one of the fairy folk helping guide her way.

As she approached Tamar's cottage, she could hear voices. On entering the croft she found that Marlea had preceded her, and must also have had the same thought that the young priest might be able to help them.

"Elspeth told me that you were learning much about our ways," Marlea was saying to Luke, who was now sitting up looking well on the path to recovery. "You must by now realize that our ways may be different from your own, but they are by no means evil."

"My mother has been arrested as a witch, Luke," Ivy burst in. "Your people are ready to hang her. You can help her. You know her ways are not evil. Please help stop them."

The young man was clearly alarmed at the news. "When did this happen, young one?" he asked, his brow wrinkled in consternation.

"But yesterday, Luke, and they say she and six others will hang for witchcraft. She helped you Luke. She healed your wounds and gave you plant medicines that made you well. Will you not now help her? Go to your people and tell them to release her. Tell them the truth."

"No!" boomed a commanding voice. It was Tamar who rose from the shadows. "Friendly though he may be, he is still a priest, and as soon as he leaves here he will do us no favors.

Soon he will lead them all here and there will be more arrests. Our village will be destroyed. No, he must not leave."

"My friends," spoke Luke with apparent sincerity. "I will help you. I..I..I made reports to the bishop... before you found me at the rock.." he stammered. "I had been watching you, all of you, for many weeks. I thought I would teach you and mend your ways. But to hang Elspeth and the others for witchcraft. No! no! That cannot be. That is wrong! So wrong. I know now from this time spent in Tamar's home that your ways are not of the devil. I have seen nothing to make me believe that. But the reports I made earlier must have made them think that Elspeth was a witch. I told them of the songs and the times I saw you dance on the heath and when you gathered at the stones. But I cannot bear the thought that they would hang people because of me. That is too, too terrible." He put his head in his hands.

Ivy sat very still and felt a flutter at her side. It was Tamar's cat, Shadow. Ivy felt like a veil was covering her sight, and then through the mist came an answer. The mist cleared.

"You shall write it down, Luke. Write it down. And I will know what you've said in the words you use, for now I can read too."

Marlea turned to her in surprise. "You, read? How? How is that possible?" said Marlea.

"It's true," said Ivy. "When I came to give Luke the salves and teas my mother sent, he would show me his book. He showed me all the letters and what they stand for. It's true. Let me show you."

Ivy reached for Luke's bible which lay next to his bed. She opened it up somewhere near the middle and slowly sounded out the words. "The...Lord...is...my...shep...herd." Marlea was astonished.

"It is true, you can read. Ivy, this is incredible." Marlea smiled with pleasure at her young friend's achievement.

"Yes and I will write a letter to the bishop telling him I was wrong and that your ways are not of the devil. That he must see to it that Elspeth and the others are released, immediately," said the young priest. "See, I will tear a page from my bible so that they will know the letter is from me. The father of my priory will know it is real as he saw me write my bible. He knows how its pages look. And you shall read it Ivy, then you will all know I am being true."

Tamar found a feather which she sharpened to a point and some strong dye that could be used as ink, and Luke started to write.

16

Elspeth sat in the darkness, using all her powers of concentration to keep herself calm and focused. She was alone in a tiny cell, with only a little straw for a bed. The room was dark and dank and smelt of sadness and suffering. Elspeth thought of the other poor souls whose final home this terrible place had been. There had been the impoverished villagers who had hunted the lord's deer because their children were starving and had been arrested and hung for it. There were poor people who had not been able to afford to pay the lord's taxes and had been locked up, thus condemning their families into further desperation.

Elspeth had not been able to talk to the other women who had been arrested the same time as her. They were from a neighboring village, and it seemed that they had all been arrested on the charge of witchcraft. Witchcraft? "What does that mean to these men?" wondered Elspeth. What was it that they did that was so evil? Those who had the power to heal were highly respected by her people. The work and effort that it takes to study and learn all the names of the plants and their properties and how to prepare them was recognized, praised and honored. It was only a few people who seemed to possess the ability to work with dreams and spells and see into the future. She had had the sight since she was a small girl, and had learned from her grandmother how to use that gift to heal and cure. Tamar and her grandmother had been old friends and when her gran had died Tamar had continued her work and teachings. "Ah yes," thought Elspeth, "I have learned much from Tamar."

She also knew that Ivy was developing the tools needed to be a great healer and worker of the craft, and had great potential. But to the Christians all these wonderful gifts were seen as evil. Was it women's power they feared? It seemed that none of the priests were women. "That must be it," thought Elspeth. "They fear us because they don't understand us and they fear our power. These are very dangerous enemies."

Suddenly the door flung open and the guard roughly threw in a bundle and a bowl of water. He spat on the ground and then slammed the door shut. His old mood was returning. Elspeth looked questioningly at the bundle, and then realized that it had a special quality and that it was indeed her cloak. A smile brightened her mood. Her friends had somehow managed to help her, and she was sure that Ivy must have assisted them.

Elspeth eagerly unwrapped the bundle and was thrilled to find her warm, familiar cloak. It was like a second skin and not only provided warmth and comfort but had many spells woven in with its threads and had been with her through many ceremonies, healings and sacred moments. Elspeth spread the cloak on the floor and lowered herself down into its midst and wrapped it around her, breathing in softly its warmth and comfort. As she breathed she recognized a fragrance, and knew where it came from. She reached down to the inner seams of the garment to the secret pocket she had woven into it so that she could hide and carry sacred ritual objects or bundles of herbs. She discovered several small packages in the hidden pocket and at once knew that this had been the work of her daughter Ivy. The fabric that the little bundles were wrapped in was from an old pinafore that Elspeth had sewn for Ivy. Elspeth held each one of the packets to her nose to discover their contents. "Ivy has done well," she smiled to herself. In one was a strong blend of herbs to calm the body and mind and promote sleep. In others were mixtures for strength and empowerment. "My young daughter is becoming very skilled at her art," spoke Elspeth to herself, with a smile.

What she spoke was true enough, but she knew only a part of Ivy's craft. Ivy was busy weaving magic elsewhere, magic of a different nature.

17

Back at Tamar's, Luke had finished his letter and Ivy had slowly and carefully read it to the impressed group that surrounded her. She faltered on a few words that were hard for her to understand, but she got the main content and was pleased that Luke had so forcefully insisted on the release of her mother. Everyone felt satisfied that the letter should be sent, and it was arranged that Tom the carpenter should travel to the church in the valley that night and under cover of darkness leave Luke's note nailed to the church door. Tamar thought that the letter should be sent but felt that it would not reach the cold hearts of the black robes and that other plans must be set.

"But this is talk for others to share in," said Tamar. "We will meet at the bower. That is a safe place to meet. We can place lookouts in case the black robes return." Tamar did not want to talk about their plans with Luke around and everyone understood that caution was essential. So Luke was left with a guard and the villagers left to summon others to the sacred bower.

Ivy went directly down to the riverside. The river and the bower that the villagers decorated had always been special places for Ivy, and now that she had experienced the message from the water it had become not just a special place but a sacred one. She sat down at the riverside and gazed into the waters. Thoughts spun through her mind about her mother and Luke and the black robes and light and dark flowed through her, fear and hope, fear and hope.

Suddenly an image appeared in the swirling pools of water. It cleared into a face, a shining woman's face. It was the face of her mother. Elspeth was calling out to her. Ivy strained to hear what her mother was saying. The image grew faint and then strong again and slowly, as she concentrated, Ivy could hear the words, "Midnight, come, bring horses." Ivy's heart pounded with joy and fear. Elspeth must have a plan to escape.

When the other villagers arrived at the riverside there was a lot of talk and discussion about what to do next. It was Tamar who called the congregated group to order. She pounded her stick on the ground and silenced them.

"Friends and neighbors, the winds of change are howling at our door. We must see to it that Elspeth is broken free and then we must make swift and rapid changes or the black robes will be back for more and more of us. Those of us with the knowledge must speak of it no more except when in the company of only those we fully trust. But know that even that is dangerous. This evil is so powerful that men will stoop to pry confessions from us by the most wicked and evil means. I have seen it in the scrying mirror. Terrible methods of torture. Many dying horrible deaths and the black robes of the Christ smothering the flames of our knowledge and wisdom."

There was a murmur of sadness, fear and disgust that trembled through the crowd, and then Ivy spoke.

"I have seen it too, grandmother. And I have also seen in the ripples of the river a message from my mother."

"Well, young Ivy. Once more you show us this growing light in you. I am glad for it young one," spoke Tamar. "And what did your mother say?"

"We are to meet her at midnight with horses. She must have a plan of escape," said Ivy boldly.

"So it shall be, then. A group must be ready and waiting and also be prepared to fight. Who will go?"

Several villagers raised their hands, amongst them of course was Ivy. But Tamar had other plans.

"No, Ivy. I want you to go home and pack your and your mother's belongings, only the most needed ones, and be prepared to leave as soon as Elspeth is freed. The black robes will be in pursuit as soon as she is discovered missing. We must flee. We must leave this area and go into hiding. I have an idea where that should be. I will leave with you as I can sense that Luke, after a valiant effort to convince his elders otherwise, will in the end betray us. So away all of you and remember my words. The times are changing, more rapidly than we can keep up with."

Ivy went home and sat for while on her cozy sheep skin bed. She stared out of the window and a tear rolled down her cheek. She had spent her whole life in this little croft, and always loved the morning sun coming in her window and the moon rising through the trees. A lump stuck in her throat and she allowed herself to sob, to cry for all the changes that were flooding into her life. The way they now had to flee and hide and not speak of their ways and their craft. The way they had to leave the village they loved and the people they knew as family. And then as Ivy's eyes stung with the pain of the depth of her sorrow, it went a step deeper and she sobbed for all the women who would not escape the torment of the black robes, and as she flung herself down onto her bed in distress, a burning log in the hearth cracked and a flame lept up from the embers, engulfing all around it.

Dreams did come to Ivy that night as she sank into sleep. She dreamt she was running through the forest, as if she was being pursued by some faceless, nameless beast. Then the dream swirled and changed and then she was in a clearing and all around her were the animals of the forest. They circled around her in protection. As she felt their closeness and comfort, a thought came to her. "There might be great changes ahead for my people, but the earth will abide forever, and our love and deep respect for her will never change." Then the animals disappeared and she was standing on a mountain top. Below her was a great valley and many, many houses and wide roads and smoke rising. She stared off into the distance and could see all the way across the valley to a hill that rose above the smoke and noise and people. At first she could not tell what was happening on top of this hill, as it was misty and shrouded in mystery. But as she stood very still and waited, breathing deep with silence, she began to see figures appear through the mist. A circle of women stood on the top of the hill and they were singing. Their dress was strange and their words sounded different, but she could just about make out what it was that they were singing. Her heart bounced in delight. It was the song she knew so well, "Earth my body. Water my blood. Air my breath and fire my spirit."

Ivy awoke with a start and felt a deep comfort within. At that moment, she knew that everything was going to be alright. It might take a while, but everything would be alright. Women's strength would never die. Somewhere, somewhere out in the future, this time would change and shift, and respect and understanding would return to the land.

She rose wearily from her bed and started to gather her strength for the job of packing her and her mother's things. She drank a cup of invigorating tea and then pulled out bags from under her bed to begin packing. Ivy realized that they might never see this little house again and that she must pack carefully in order to have everything that they would need for their new life. There were some things that could never be replaced, things that had been passed down through the generations in her family and the things that were special or magical because they were used in ritual or ceremony. So Ivy dragged the trunk down from the rafters and with a deep breath opened it up. Inside was the staff with the amethyst eyes that Elspeth had used at the stone circle ceremony, and many little bags of different herbs and mixtures. Ivy gathered them all up and put them in a large woven bag.

"It must nearly be midnight," she thought to herself, and lowered her head in concentration to send thoughts of courage and success to her mother. "Set my mother free!" she called out loud.

18

Elspeth had a plan. She had seen the jailer pace back and forth outside her cell and was beginning to get a sense of what he was like. She thought that she could probably tempt him in some way so as to lure him from his post. He was a sullen fellow and seemed to care not for the job he was told to do. Elspeth could hear him muttering and mumbling under his breath about the long hours he had to work and the low wages he received. He was always hungry and never had a break from his duties so he could not leave his post and go and get a meal. Maybe she could tempt him with some warm brew she could concoct from the herbs that Ivy had sent in the cloak. She knew that she could also work some soothing magic that would lure him into trusting her.

Elspeth gathered her cloak around her and fell into trance. She worked all her thoughts towards the direction of the guard, imagining him softening towards her and feeling them both captives of the powerful lords who controlled the area. With all her strength and powers of concentration she summoned his energy.

When she was ready she spoke. "Hey fellow. I can see that you too are cold and hungry. Our masters care not who suffers." The man swung round with a scowl and grimace. But as his eyes connected with Elspeth's he softened. She reminded him of his sister, who he had not seen for years.

"Aye," he growled. "We neither gets no pity from them."

"Well, sir," said Elspeth, summoning all her powers, "I have some herbs in my pocket that will make a wonderful brew. If you hand me the water jug you have hanging by the fire I will mix us some tea."

The man looked tempted, but caught himself and snarled, "And why should I trust you, witch?"

Elspeth was quick to respond, "Well what harm can come of it? It will taste mighty good, and if you fear mischief then you can watch me drink first."

The guard could not imagine what harm there would be in that, so he agreed. He carried the jug of hot water into the cell. Elspeth removed a bundle of herbs from her pocket, and sprinkled them into the steaming water. "It must steep a while," she said to the man. He snarled and slouched down on the floor to wait. After a few minutes Elspeth announced that the tea was ready and lifted the pot to her lips to drink. The mixture was strong and delicious and she knew that she could drink it without ill-effect, as she had already taken a potion from the secret stash that Ivy had hidden in her cloak that would counteract the effects of the strong herbs in this brew. To her it

80

was delicious and invigorating, but to him it would cause instant sleep. She took several drafts and then handed him the jug. He eyed her suspiciously for a few minutes and decided it would be alright for him to drink some of it. Elspeth kept her eyes focused intensely on him and her purpose. He drained the rest of the brew in one hearty series of gulps. His eyes danced and his face flushed. He enjoyed the warmth and flavor of the concoction.

"That tasted delicious... Mistress... and makes me... feel good ... all... over." His words began to fade as he began to melt into sleep. Soon his eyes were closed and he was snoring peacefully.

Elspeth was quick to act. She grabbed the ring of keys from his belt and unlocked her cell door. She then quickly locked it from the other side so as to lock him in should he awake before she had released the others. She then rushed down the passage to the cells where the other women were locked up. It took a few precious minutes to find the correct key for each lock, but she managed to get the other doors open and cried to the women to make haste. They ran from the jail into the dark night. Elspeth hoped that her friends had received her message from Ivy and would be waiting with horses. They ran and ran, and then through the darkness she could see figures approaching. Her heart pounded. "Please let it be them," she whispered under her breath. And indeed it was. Out of the misty forest appeared Marlea and the others with extra horses. One woman decided to continue on foot to her village, some sped off in another direction and Elspeth jumped on the back of Marlea's horse and with joy in her heart, galloped towards home.

19

From inside the cottage, Ivy could hear a commotion going on outside. She was both excited and scared. Was it Elspeth returning or some new catastrophe? She ran to the window and could make out dozens of men on horseback riding through the village. There were screams and shouts and Ivy rushed outside to see what was going on. It was the black robes. They had returned. The head black robe who had first appeared to warn them had someone captured with a rope and was dragging him around in circles. Another black robe was beating a woman with a stick and screaming things at her. These two people were held hostage and the other villagers kept back in anguish in case their actions would enrage the black robes even further. Ivy could make out the words, "Tell us where he is! Tell us now, or..." The chaotic crowd started to file towards the forest and Ivy guessed that the captured villagers had told of the whereabouts of the young priest, Luke, and were leading the other priests to him out of fear for their lives.

Ivy quickly started thinking what she should do when the thunder of hooves was heard behind her. Her heart skipped a beat. Was it the black robes come for her? She swung around, but instead of seeing the dreadful figures in black, she saw the faces of Elspeth and Marlea smiling down at her from the horse in front. "Quick, Ivy, gather our things, we must away!" cried Elspeth. As she spoke another figure appeared from the darkness. It was Tamar, out of breath and staggering. "They are upon us. We must flee," she gasped.

Elspeth, Tamar and Ivy ran to the cottage and gathered their bags, and then ran back out to the waiting villagers. "Marlea, my friend and companion," spoke Elspeth. "I shall miss you. Keep safe and remember this, the knowledge lives on in our hearts. No one will ever be able to remove it. We are part of an ancient circle. Take care, dearest one, we will meet in our dreams and at the scrying pool." With hugs and farewells, Tamar, Elspeth and Ivy set off across the heath, heading north and west into another land and another time, as the first of the morning's color appeared on the horizon and the light of dawn began to spread across the sky.

Meanwhile, back in the forest, the crowd had arrived at Tamar's door. The guards were overpowered by the many black robes and their followers, and the head black robe burst open the door to Tamar's cottage. Luke was cowering inside. "So!" boomed the stern voice of the head priest, as he pulled a piece of paper from his pocket and waved it in the air. "So! You want us to believe that these witches and devil worshippers are good, kindly folk? Is that it my young innocent boy?" As he spoke he threw the letter in Luke's face. "My dear boy, you are sadly confused. These witches have fed you lies, and made you into one of them have they? Well, you know how God deals with sinners. You will be punished my boy, until all the sin is beaten out of you. Do you hear me?" he screamed.

Luke put his face in his hands and wept. "Father," he mumbled. "I sinned not. They fed me and healed my wounds. I cannot think them evil."

"Enough!" boomed the voice of the head black robe. "The decree of his majesty King James is that all witchcraft must be eliminated from the face of God's earth. Dare you to contradict his majesty the king and what is written in the holiest of books, the bible? My dear boy, you are sadly disillusioned."

He grabbed Luke, who was still sobbing, by the arm and pushed him out of the door to the awaiting crowd. Luke was helped up onto a horse, and the black robes prepared to depart. "But we shall be back," threatened the head black robe. "We shall hunt out all the devils and demons of this village and bring you all to god!" With that they left.

20

Two years later Elspeth, Tamar and Ivy were feeling settled in their new homes. They had headed for a small village in the north lands where Tamar's cousin lived. It was a long and treacherous journey, but with the help of kind folk they met along the way, they arrived at the village after several weeks of traveling.

Tamar's cousin and her friends helped them repair an old deserted croft and slowly the place was transformed into home. The three women slowly adapted to their new life and kept their knowledge of power and magic very secret, as there was always fear of witch-hunters coming and snooping around for signs of the old faith. Many villagers decided that it would serve them best to openly pretend to be converting to the Christian faith, but in their hearts and in their secret meetings the old ways prevailed.

Ivy met a few people who had also learned to read and write, and so she was able to develop her skills further and her childish scrawl and limited knowledge gradually turned into a beautiful script that used elaborate lettering and many words of description and detail. Ivy loved to read and write and was always overjoyed when someone brought her a new text. The words that she had heard at the river near her old home were not forgotten, and Ivy had begun to write down much of what she learnt from Tamar and her mother, Elspeth. They all knew that this was a very dangerous thing to do, so Ivy had found an old metal box at the market one day and decided to use it to store her notes in. She dug a hole in amongst the roots of an ancient oak tree, and there the box was hidden while she was not working on her notes.

Stories often reached town of how things were going in other parts of the country from traveling minstrels and merchants. Occasionally Ivy heard tell of things in her own village. The news was very sad often, because there were stories of horrendous violence against people that the Christians called witches. It was told that many people were hung and in some cases burned at the stake for witchcraft, but that these people were not evil people, but the old women midwives and healers, the herbalists and doctors. Some men died too, but it seemed that most of the victims were women.

One night Ivy and Elspeth were sitting at their hearth, enjoying the warmth of the logs crackling on the fire, when there was a knock at the door. Elspeth peeked through the window to see who was there. It was one of the villagers. Elspeth hesitantly opened the door.

"Good evenin' Mistress," said Tom, who was the village blacksmith. "I am sorry to trouble you, but there's this man at the inn asking after you and Miss Ivy. He said he had a message for you from your old home. He seemed like a good man, so I said I'd fetch you, thinking you may want news from afar."

"What can this mean?" wondered Elspeth. "Perhaps it is a message from Marlea."

"Thank you, Tom," she said to the man. "We shall come at once."

When Ivy and Elspeth entered the inn it was full of noise and smoke as the villagers were enjoying their evening company. Tom pointed to a figure who was huddled by the fire in a big brown cloak. As Ivy neared the person her heart skipped a beat. It was a man she knew. It was Luke, the young black robe. She grasped her mother's hand and prepared to bolt. Had the young man hunted them out and was come to arrest them? But as she turned, there was Tamar.

"It is alright, Ivy," Tamar spoke softly. "What we have here is a changed man, a black robe no more."

Luke looked up and Ivy could tell from his face that this was a man in deep suffering. Elspeth, Ivy and Tamar sat down next to him. "I am so glad to see you both, alive and well," said Luke, his voice low and cracked. "I am on my way across the ocean to Eire. I am to go to the sea port tonight. I am so glad I finally found you. I was so afraid they had found you and, and, that you had suffered the fate of so, so many others." He faltered and Tamar handed him a goblet of mead to give him strength. "I just needed to see you alive, and to tell you how sorry I am for what happened to your friends and village. Those men are like beasts, and I will have none of their kind. I go in search of people who live true to Christ's teachings, not use them to further sickness and death and their own merciless power. Last week," he faltered again, "last week Brother Pius and the others arrested Marlea, June and several others of the village, and erected a scaffold on the heath and hung them all." He stopped and sobbed, putting his head in his hands. Ivy clutched her mother. What terrible news this was. Luke continued, between the sobs, "I tried to stop them. But they had broken me. They beat me and imprisoned me and told me I was bewitched for saying that you were good kindly folk. So I ran away when I could, and will return there no more."

"My boy," said Tamar. "May you find peace where you travel. Thank you for bringing us this news. This insanity abounds in many other villages and I believe in other lands, too. But go now, and speak no more of what you learned of us and our healing ways. For this is a dangerous time, and none of us are safe."

"Before I go I want to give you something," he said reaching for his bag. "I learned how to make parchment and bind books at the priory and this I made for you, Ivy." He handed her a beautifully bound book with a silver button that fastened it. "I hope you write many things in it, and I hope that one day we can all make peace and learn to learn to live as brothers and sisters, not as enemies. Now I must go."

Ivy gave Luke a hug and thanked him sincerely for his gift, and the young man took his leave.

"The spirit of the river told me to speak, write and tell all, mother, " said Ivy as they walked home, their hearts sad at the news of the death of their dear friends. "This book Luke gave me shall be the place where I write it all down. I will write the story of our people, our rituals, medicine and lore. And I will also tell our story of the witch hunts and the oppression of our people and their ways. People like our dear friend, Marlea who died at the hands of the black robes. Then I shall bury the book in the metal box deep in the ground. Then one day, I have seen it in my dreams, there will come a time when there is not so much fear and hatred of the ancient ways by those in power and someone will find the book and learn of the history of our people. Once again the old rituals will be performed, the songs chanted, the herbs used to heal. There will come a time. There will come a time..."

It was in the darkest time of the year, near the winter solstice, when Ivy had finished writing the book. Ivy, Elspeth and Tamar met in secret one night under a spreading oak. They cast a circle and sang some of the old songs of their people. They left some offerings to the forest and the earth mother and then Ivy took her book and placed it in its metal box and put it into a deep hole. As she filled the hole with soil, she spoke.

"I bury this book deep in the heart of my mother the earth and ask that she keep it safe so that others of her children might share its wisdom. We are all part of an ancient circle. May the circle never be broken. So mote it be."

As the three women headed back towards their new home in the moonlight, a deep peace settled in their hearts.

THE END